Hello, Family Members,

Learning to read is one of the most important accomplishments of early childhood. **Hello Reader!** b children become skilled readers wh readers learn to read by remember like "the," "is," and "and"; by using p words; and by interpreting picture a.... provide both the stories children enjoy and the structure they need to read fluently and independently. Here are suggestions for helping your child.

- Have your child think about a word he or she does not recognize right away. Provide hints such as "Let's see if we know the sounds" and "Have we read other words like this one?"
- Encourage your child to use phonics skills to sound out new words.
- Provide the word for your child when more assistance is needed so that he or she does not struggle and the experience of reading with you is a positive one.
- Encourage your child to have fun by reading with a lot of expression . . . like an actor!

I do hope that you and your child enjoy this book.

> —Francie Alexander
> Reading Specialist,
> Scholastic's Learning Ventures

Activity Pages

In the back of the book are skill-building activities. These are designed to give children further reading and comprehension practice and to provide added enjoyment. Offer help with directions as needed and encourage your child to have FUN with each activity.

Game Cards

In the middle of the book are eight pairs of game cards. These are designed to help your child become more familiar with words in the book and to play fun games.

- Have your child use the word cards to find matching words in the story. Then have him or her use the picture cards to find matching words in the story.
- Play a matching game. Here's how: Place the cards face up. Have your child match words to pictures. Once the child feels confident matching words to pictures, put cards face down. Have the child lift one card, then lift a second card to see if both match. If the cards match, the child can keep them. If not, place the cards face down once again.
Keep going until he or she finds all matches.

To Alice, Jean, Joanne, and lunch
—M.S.

For Samantha and Stephanie,
my two treasures
—J.S.

No part of this publication may be reproduced, or stored in a retrieval system, or transmitted in any form or by any means, electronic, mechanical, photocopying, recording, or otherwise, without written permission of the publisher. For information regarding permission, write to Scholastic Inc., Attention: Permissions Department, 555 Broadway, New York, NY 10012.

ISBN 0-439-17933-5

Text copyright © 2001 by Mary Serfozo.
Illustrations copyright © 2001 by Jeffrey Scherer.
All rights reserved. Published by Scholastic Inc.
SCHOLASTIC, HELLO READER, CARTWHEEL BOOKS and associated logos
are trademarks and/or registered trademarks of Scholastic Inc.

Library of Congress Cataloging-in-Publication Data

Serfozo, Mary.
         The big bug dug / by Mary Serfozo; illustrated by Jeffrey Scherer.
         p.   cm. — (My first hello reader!)
      "Cartwheel Books."
      "With game cards."
         Summary: Looking for a quiet place to sleep, a big bug digs down past a snake, a slug, a worm, and down even more.
         ISBN 0-439-17933-5
         [1. Insects — Fiction. 2. Animals — Fiction. 3. Stories in rhyme.] I. Scherer, Jeffrey, ill. II. Title. III. Series.
      PZ8.3.S4688 Bi 2001
      [E] — dc20   00-029720

12 11 10 9 8 7 6 5   02 03 04 05

Printed in the U.S.A.   23
First printing, April 2001

The Big Bug Dug

by Mary Serfozo
Illustrated by Jeffrey Scherer

My First Hello Reader!
With Game Cards

SCHOLASTIC INC.
Cartwheel BOOKS ®

New York   Toronto   London   Auckland   Sydney
Mexico City   New Delhi   Hong Kong

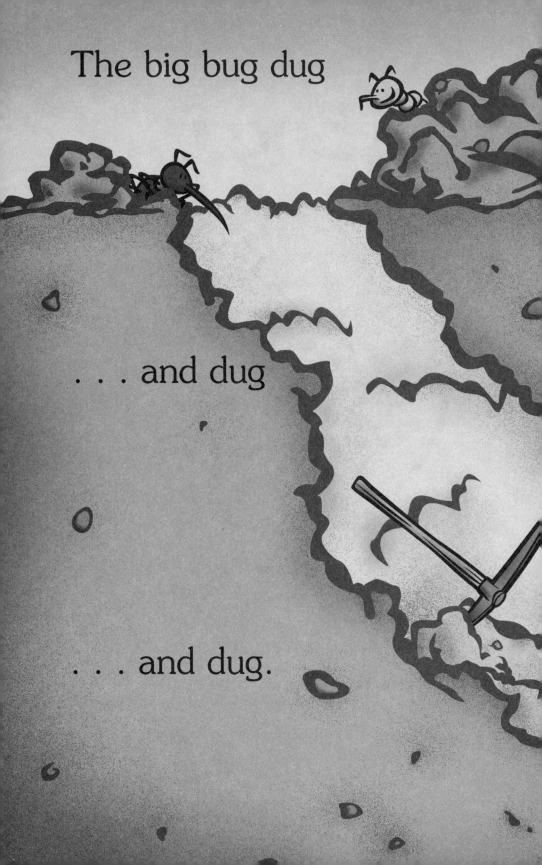

The big bug dug

. . . and dug

. . . and dug.

Down in the dirt,
the big bug dug.

Dug past a snake.

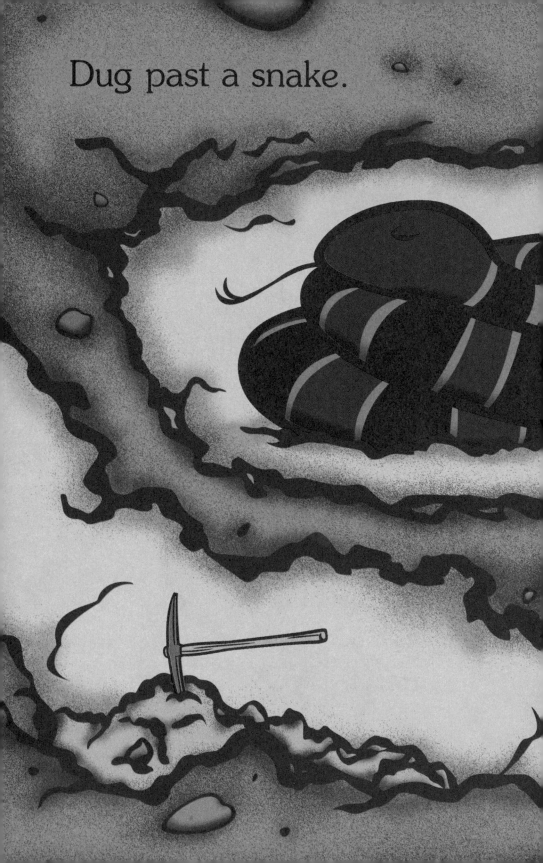

Dug past
a slug.

Down past a worm,

the big bug dug.

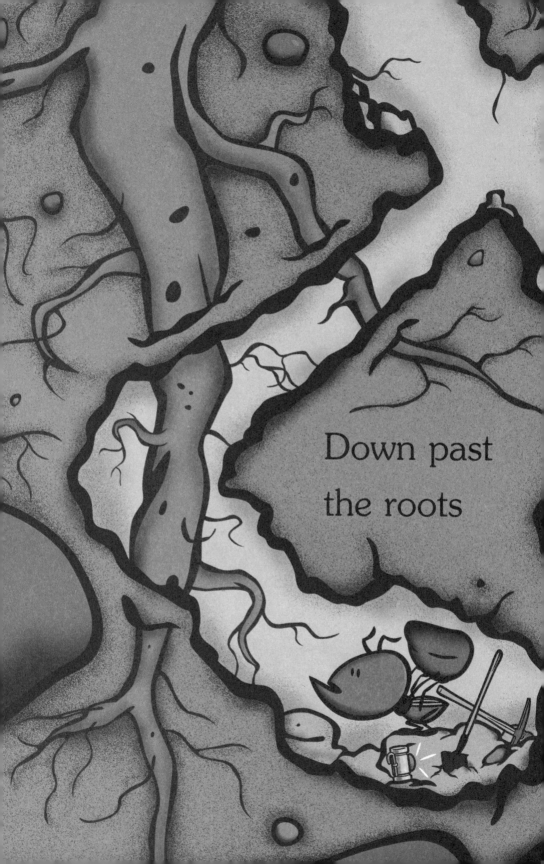

Down past

the roots

and gopher holes.

Down past the rocks.

Down past the moles.

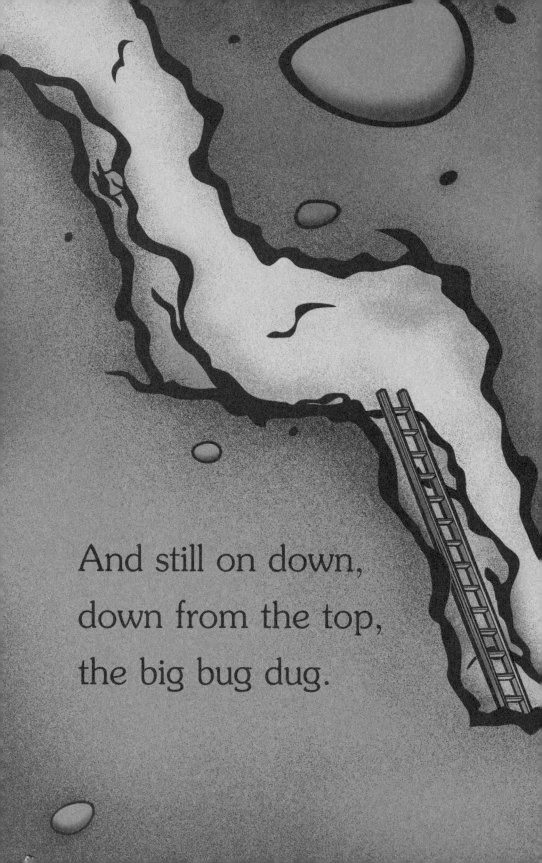

And still on down,
down from the top,
the big bug dug.

Where would he stop?

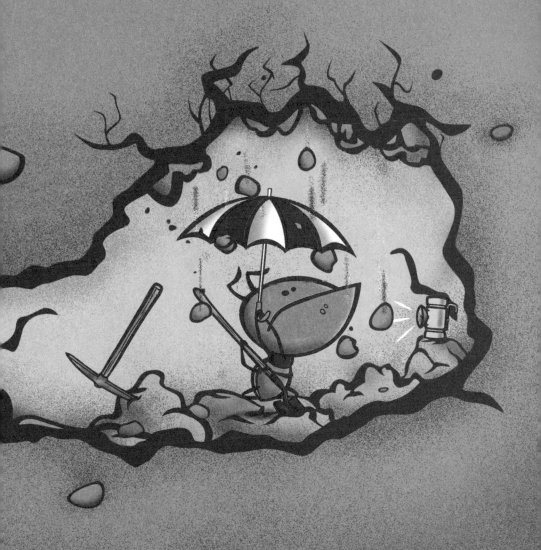

He didn't stop
for lunch or nap.

He didn't stop
to check the map.

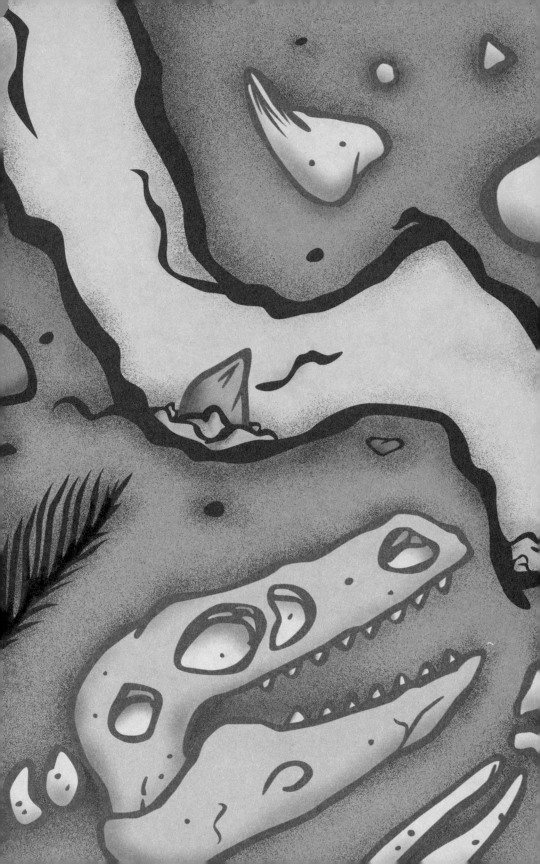

Just dug on down,
that big old bug.

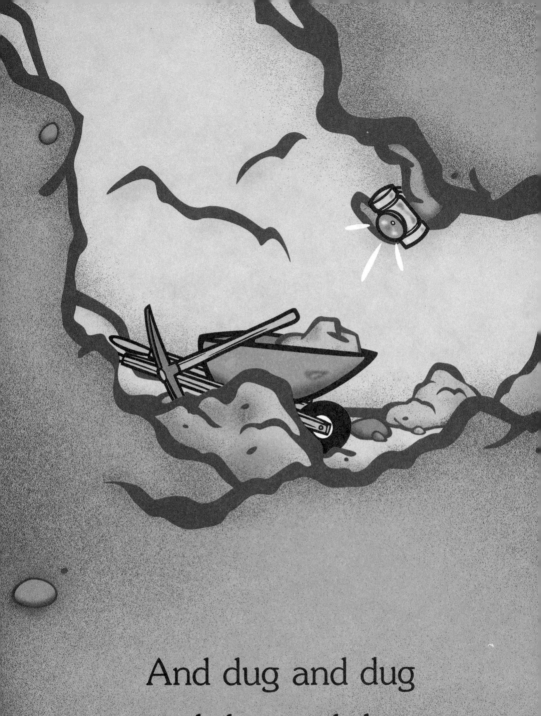

And dug and dug
and dug and dug.

Until he met . . .

no one at all.

No moles, no gophers
came to call.

No worms, no slugs,
no sounds to hear.

Then the big bug said,
"At last—I'm here!

"No bug should have
to dig so deep
to find a quiet
place to sleep!"

ZZZZZZZzzzzz

Opposites

Opposite words mean something completely different from each other. For example, **high** is the opposite of **low**. Draw a line to match each word with its opposite.

top	**little**
down	**go**
big	**bottom**
stop	**up**

Surprise! Surprise!

Connect the dots from A to Z for a surprise.

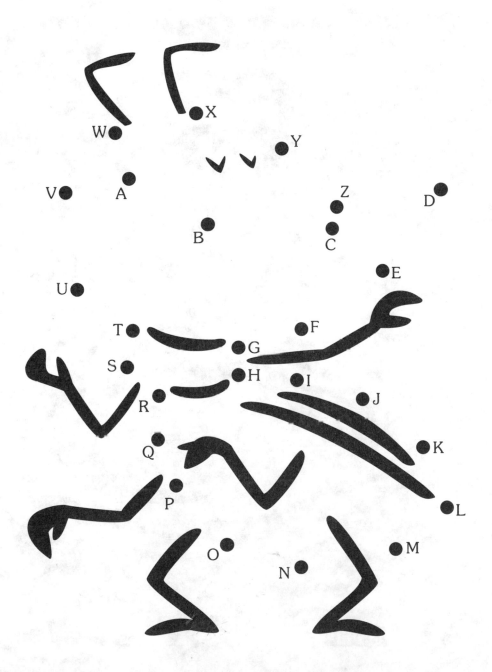

A-maze-ing Bug

Help the big bug find
a quiet place to sleep.

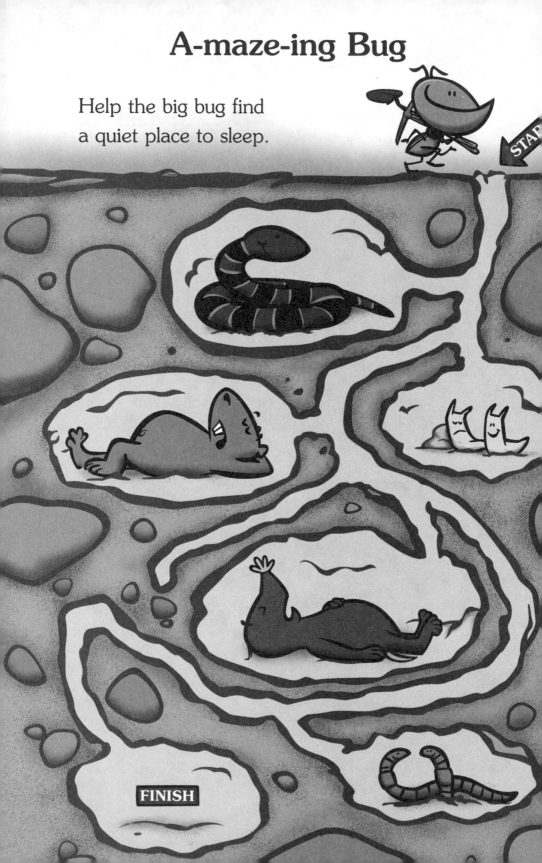

A Rhyme for You

Fun and **sun** are words that rhyme. In each row, circle the picture that rhymes with the word.

dug

rocks

map

hear

call

A Buggy Word Find

The word BUG is hidden in this word find
puzzle ten times. Look up, down, and across.
See if you can find them all.

```
B U G B B G
U G U U G B
G B B U G U
U B U G U G
B U G B B B
```

Fill in the Blanks

Where did the big bug dig?

He dug down in the **d__rt**.

 What did the big bug pass?

He dug past a **w__r__**.

What was the big bug looking for?

He was looking for a quiet place

to **s__e__p**.

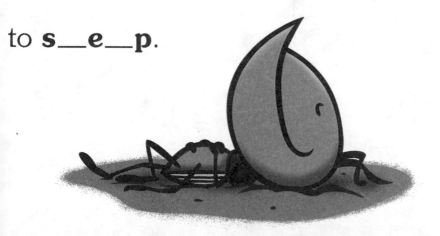

ANSWERS

Opposites

top — bottom
down — up
big — little
stop — go

Surprise! Surprise!

A-maze-ing Bug

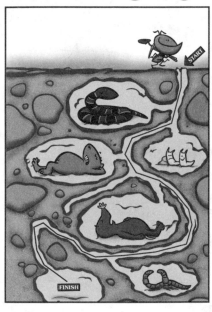

A Rhyme for You

dug
rocks
map
hear
call

A Buggy Word Find

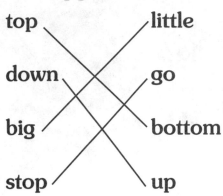

Fill in the Blanks

He dug down in the d**i**rt.

He dug past a w**orm**.

He was looking for a quiet place to s**lee**p.